THE SLEEPING GIANTESS WAKES UP

Written and illustrated by
CLARE ROSENFIELD

THE SLEEPING GIANTESS WAKES UP

Published by Gatekeeper Press
2167 Stringtown Rd, Suite 109
Columbus, OH 43123-2989
www.GatekeeperPress.com

Copyright © 2022 by Clare Rosenfield

All rights reserved. Neither this book, nor any parts within it may be sold or reproduced in any form or by any electronic or mechanical means, including information storage and retrieval systems, without permission in writing from the author. The only exception is by a reviewer, who may quote short excerpts in a review.

ISBN (paperback): 9781662927928

Once upon a time, there was a sleeping Giantess who spread her body across the entire world. Her legs were in the south, her head and neck were in the north, her right arm was in the east and her left arm was in the west. She was sprawled out everywhere so that when she snored, the sound echoed throughout all of space, and when she changed positions, everything underneath her and on her shook.

Actually, all the people who lived on Planet Earth did not realize that this was truly the body of Mother Earth and they were all living in and on it. There wasn't anywhere else for them to live and yet no one knew it. All they knew was that they lived in different spots and locations. But no one recognized that Mother Earth was the sleeping Giantess, and their only home.

Because of this, the people were fighting over their space, fighting over their possessions, fighting over their ideas, and fighting over who gets what and when and how much. This made the sleeping Giantess have a very bad sleep. She had nightmares. She had aches and pains. She had restlessness. But she did not wake up.

She did not wake up for several billions of years. She was the sleeping Giantess but the real reason no one knew about her was because each person thought that each was separate. No one realized that each of them was connected with one another and that in fact, each of them was intimately related with the sleeping Giantess, because they were made of her earthen soil and sacred waters.

2

She was their first mother, Mother Earth herSelf. After being formed of her body elements, everything came from Her to support their lives—the vegetables from the gardens, the water from the clean streams, the grains from the fields, the fruit that grew from trees and vines, the seeds, nuts, and medicinal plants that abounded in rainforests and elsewhere.

Until one day there were two children who decided to walk from one end of the earth to the other. They took each other's hand and began to walk. As they walked, they got into a nice rhythm of breathing and walking, walking and breathing. As they were breathing, they put their attention in their heart. Breathing into the heart, breathing out from the heart. It was so relaxing and easy that it allowed them to walk for a long time without getting tired.

4

Then they added something extra. They breathed in love, they breathed out appreciation. They breathed in happiness, they breathed out compassion. They breathed in goodness, they breathed out care. They breathed in peace, they breathed out calmness. When their caring became so big and vast and deep and wide, it became a caring for the whole, the whole world.

And that was the key to waking up the Sleeping Giantess.

As she opened her eyes, she stopped dreaming, she stopped feeling restless, she stopped being uncomfortable, she stopped having nightmares.

As she opened his eyes, all of a sudden everyone saw each other.

Everyone recognized something very important.

They were all part of that one body of the Giantess. Once the Giantess woke up, everyone woke up. Everyone realized they were united in that one body and that made all the difference.

They stopped fighting and competing. They stopped wanting what the other one had. They stopped yelling and screaming at each other. They stopped hurting each other. Instead, they cared.

They looked around and smiled at each other. They hugged. They said Thank You! They felt happy and connected. They were not all alone anymore. They saw the truth—they were one big body of humanity and all living creatures too. They were part of the stars and the galaxies and the cosmos.

And they could breathe in love, compassion, goodness, appreciation, thankfulness, and joy at the same time, and they could breathe out this magnificent attitude at the same time.

And when they looked up, the sun was smiling, the stars were twinkling, the moon was thanking them, and the space was imprinted with love-prints everywhere. And that is the way the world shifted into an awake love-fest of oneness. The Sleeping Giantess was now the Wide Awake Giantess and everyone could recognize that She was Mother Earth after all. And She was happier than She had ever been.

ABOUT THE AUTHOR
CLARE S. ROSENFIELD

Since the age of thirteen, when Clare was asked by her teacher to write her career notebook, she has been fulfilling her dream of writing and illustrating her own books, both poetry and children's stories. Her poetry and verse narratives include: dance upon the winds swept cloudless, ROLL ON GREAT EARTH, Tall Grasses of Woods Hole & Other Summery Poems, The Call of Mother Earth: How a Being of Light Draws Forth Humanity's Response, Nameless One of Splendor: Her Sacred Arts of Creation, Ninsun: Wise Mother of Gilgamesh and Your Inmost Tree of Life: An Invitation. Her children's stories are: SUN-CHILD, Seven Meditations for Children, The Story of Liliana: A Brave Indigenous Child, The Little Girl who wanted to be a Tree, and more to come.

Clare has also co-authored Ten Lives of the Buddha: Siamese Temple Paintings and Jataka Tales while living in Thailand fifty years ago, wrote a biography in the 1980's called Gurudev Shree Chitrabhanu: A Man with a Vision, edited two of his books of talks: Sense Beyond the Senses and Twelve Facets of Reality: The Jain Path to Freedom, co-authored with his wife Pramoda Chitrabhanu To Light One Candle: Prayers for

<u>Peace from the Jain, Buddhist, and Hindu traditions</u>, and co-authored with Linda Segall <u>Reverence for All Life and Vegetarianism</u>.

Besides writing, painting, harp-playing, and meditating, Clare's greatest joy is being with her six grandchildren, from ages 12 to 22, each of whom is creative artistically, musically, and educationally, in fields such as public health, restorative justice, the behavioral sciences, and history.

As President of the Global Healing Foundation, Clare has a longtime interest in awakening humanity to our collective urgent need to protect Mother Earth, her rainforests, her healthy soil, her rivers and streams, her wildlife, her biodiversity, and the people who are equally dedicated to taking care not to destroy our only home, our sacred planet, for our mutual survival. That includes environmentally conscious sacred activists, indigenous people standing up for their rights and the rights of Mother Earth, and all who would speak out for the survival and thrival of our future generations. She wants everyone to feel held in the loving arms of our Mother Earth. (Contact: crosenfield9@gmail.com; www.contacthealing.com; www.globalhealingfoundation.org)